Dear mouse frien[illegible]
welcome to the wo[illegible] of

4
5
6
2
1
11
3
13
12
PIZZA
14
15
20
22
16
21
30
23
31
32
33

The Editorial Staff of
The Rodent's Gazette

1. Linda Thinslice
2. Sweetie Cheesetriangle
3. Ratella Redfur
4. Soya Mousehao
5. Cheesita de la Pampa
6. Mouseanna Mousetti
7. Yale Youngmouse
8. Toni Tinypaw
9. Tina Spicytail
10. Maximilian Mousemower
11. Valerie Vole
12. Trap Stilton
13. Branwen Musclemouse
14. Zeppola Zap
15. Merenguita Gingermouse
16. Ratsy O'Shea
17. Rodentrick Roundrat
18. Teddy von Muffler
19. Thea Stilton
20. Erronea Misprint
21. Pinky Pick
22. Ya-ya O'Cheddar
23. Mousella MacMouser
24. Kreamy O'Cheddar
25. Blasco Tabasco
26. Toffie Sugarsweet
27. Tylerat Truemouse
28. Larry Keys
29. Michael Mouse
30. Geronimo Stilton
31. Benjamin Stilton
32. Briette Finerat
33. Raclette Finerat

Geronimo Stilton
A learned and brainy mouse; editor of *The Rodent's Gazette*

Thea Stilton
Geronimo's sister and special correspondent at *The Rodent's Gazette*

Trap Stilton
An awful joker; Geronimo's cousin and owner of the store Cheap Junk for Less

Benjamin Stilton
A sweet and loving nine-year-old mouse; Geronimo's favorite nephew

Geronimo Stilton
THE MONA MOUSA CODE
PUFFIN

PUFFIN BOOKS

Published by the Penguin Group
Penguin Books Ltd, 80 Strand, London WC2R 0RL, England
Penguin Group (USA) Inc., 375 Hudson Street, New York, New York 10014, USA
Penguin Group (Canada), 90 Eglinton Avenue East, Suite 700, Toronto, Ontario, Canada M4P 2Y3
(a division of Pearson Penguin Canada Inc.)
Penguin Ireland, 25 St Stephen's Green, Dublin 2, Ireland (a division of Penguin Books Ltd)
Penguin Group (Australia), 707 Collins Street, Melbourne, Victoria 3008, Australia
(a division of Pearson Australia Group Pty Ltd)
Penguin Books India Pvt Ltd, 11 Community Centre, Panchsheel Park, New Delhi – 110 017, India
Penguin Group (NZ), 67 Apollo Drive, Rosedale, Auckland 0632, New Zealand
(a division of Pearson New Zealand Ltd)
Penguin Books (South Africa) (Pty) Ltd, Block D, Rosebank Office Park, 181 Jan Smuts Avenue,
Parktown North, Gauteng 2193, South Africa

Penguin Books Ltd, Registered Offices: 80 Strand, London WC2R 0RL, England

www.puffinbooks.com
www.geronimostilton.com/uk

English-language edition first published in Great Britain by Scholastic Children's Books 2007
This edition published in Great Britain by Puffin Books 2014
001

Text by Geronimo Stilton
Cover illustration by Andrew Farley
Illustrations by Matt Wolf (idea), Lorenzo Chiavini and Michele Dall'Orso (realization)
Graphics by Merenguita Gingermouse, Marina Bonanno and Beatrice Sciascia
Special thanks to Tracey West
English translation by Joan L. Giurdanella
Interior layout by Kay Petronio

Original title: *Il sorriso di Monna Topisa*
Based on an original idea by Elisabetta Dami

Stilton is the name of a famous English cheese. It is a registered trademark of the Stilton Cheesemakers' Association. For more information go to www.stiltoncheese.com

Printed in Italy by Printer Trento S.r.l.

British Library Cataloguing in Publication Data
A CIP catalogue record for this book is available from the British Library

ISBN: 978–0–141–35400–2

I Am Not a Brave Mouse

"Mouse hole, sweet mouse hole," I said with a sigh. It was late at night, and I was glad to be home.

But as I scampered up the steps, I immediately knew **SOMETHING WAS WRONG**.

Why was the door open? I knew I had locked it that morning. And Why was there a light on in the upstairs window? I always turn off the lights when I leave the house.

I tiptoed through the door, quiet as a mouse. I padded down the dark hallway. I stopped at the kitchen door and poked my snout around the corner. The fridge was wide open!

Someone must have broken in. I was sure

I can't even go to a scary movie without turning as pale as a slice of Swiss cheese.

of it. I shuddered. I must admit, I am a bit of a 'fraidy mouse. I can't even go to a scary movie without turning as pale as a slice of Swiss cheese. After I watched *Nightmare on Cat Street,* I couldn't sleep for a week!

Suddenly, just like in the movies, a shadow appeared on the kitchen wall. Then I heard strange sounds. Someone was gurgling, munching, chomping. . . .

I slowly backed away from the door. But the shadow moved toward me.

My heart was pounding like a rat who'd just run a mousathon. I DASHED behind the curtains to hide.

Would the intruder find me?

My Fifteenth-Century Rinds!

A greasy hand moved the curtain aside. Mouse bumps broke out all over my body. I was about to be snout-to-snout with the intruder! And it was . . . my cousin Trap?!

"Hi, there!" he shouted. "Aren't you happy to see me, Cousinkins?"

Happy? I had been SCARED out of my wits! "Y-y-you sneaked into my house!" I squeaked.

"Don't get your fur frazzled, Geronimoid," Trap said. He had crumbs all over his shirt and a piece of pie in one paw. "I was passing by and saw that one of the windows was open. So I said to myself, why not pay good old Germeister a surprise visit?"

"Surprise visit!" I cried. "You almost gave me a heart attack!"

Trap chuckled. "You need to relax, Gerry Berry," he said. "You're as nervous as a rat at a cat convention."

Trap wiped his snout on my velvet curtain. "I must say, this cheese-and-pickle pie is scrumptious. It melts in the mouth!"

"**PAWS OFF!**" I shrieked. "That is a very old curtain."

"I don't mind if it's old. Any rag will do," Trap SMIRKED, wiping his snout again.

Then, before I could stop him, Trap parked his chubby body in an expensive antique chair.

SLURP!

It had cost me as much as a year's worth of cheddar.

"NO!" I screamed.

Too late. The chair smashed into a dozen pieces. Trap crashed to the floor.

"My chair!" I yelled.

As he fell, Trap knocked down a glass display cabinet. It held my treasured collection of antique cheese rinds. They spilled out onto the floor.

"My fifteenth-century rinds!" I moaned.

Trap bit off another piece of pie. "Don't you want to know why I'm here?" he asked, spraying crumbs all over me.

I couldn't take it anymore. "I don't want to know," I said. "**GET OUT!** And do me a favor — eat with your snout shut!"

Tsk Tsk "*Tsk, tsk.* You really are too fond of your antiques," Trap said. "Shouldn't you be more worried about me? After all, I am your own fur and blood. Well, never mind. I'll tell you my news anyway."

Trap winked at me. Then he leaned over and whispered in my ear. "I have a great story for you. For that little news rag you put out."

I was insulted. "You mean my newspaper, *The Rodent's Gazette*? The most respected newspaper on Mouse Island?"

"Whatever," Trap said. "I've got a scoop for you that will make everyone's whiskers stand on end. I can tell you this much. It's about Mouse Island's most famouse painting . . . the *Mona Mousa*!"

Mona Mousa...

My Name Is Stilton, Geronimo Stilton

My cousin might be annoying, but he does have a good nose for a story. An article about the *Mona Mousa* was the cat's whiskers.

You see, I know a thing or two about good stories. I run a publishing house, the Stilton Publishing Company. We put out *The Rodent's Gazette.* Oh, silly me, I haven't introduced myself. My name is Stilton, *Geronimo Stilton*.

I told my cousin to meet me at my office the next morning. Eight o'clock sharp.

Twelve hours later, Trap **bounced** into the office without bothering to knock (as usual). He rested his greasy paws on my desk (as usual). Then he squeaked with his mouth

full (as usual), "Let's talk!"

I noticed ***with disgust*** that Trap was munching on something (as usual). This time it was a multi-decker sandwich. Only Trap could eat such a super-stuffed sandwich so early in the morning!

"I'll give you the dirt on the *Mona Mousa* affair," Trap began. "When the story hits big, we'll split the profits equally: **70** percent for me and **30** percent for you."

"You call that equal?" I asked, miffed.

"Is money all you care about?" Trap grumbled. "All right. Out of the goodness of my heart, we'll do **60** percent for me and **40** percent for you."

Just then, the door to my office flew open. My sister, Thea, the special correspondent for *The Rodent's Gazette,* came **ROARING** in on her motorcycle.

"I heard what you two were talking about," Thea said. "I'll tell you how to split

the profits: *one-third* for me and one-third for each of you."

"Why should we cut you a slice of the profits?" Trap demanded.

Thea leaned on the desk, smiling slyly. "Because I know something about the *Mona Mousa* that you don't," she sang, *taunting us.*

That didn't surprise me one bit. If something exciting is happening on Mouse Island, Thea is usually the first one to hear about it.

Trap frowned. "ALL RIGHT," he mumbled. "We'll split the profits three ways. But I get to keep the television rights, and the movie rights, and . . ."

Thea folded her arms firmly. "No deal, Trap. We divide *everything* equally, or I won't squeak."

Trap sighed. "Fine, but only because I am a true *gentlemouse*. Let's shake on it!"

Just then, a voice rang out. "ME, TOO! ME, TOO!"

I looked down to see Benjamin, my nine-year-old nephew, tugging at my sleeve.

"Too late! There are no extra shares!" Trap said quickly.

"You can keep the money," Benjamin said. "I don't care about that!" Benjamin looked up at me. "Please, Uncle Geronimo. Let me help you. I want us to be together!"

I was moved to tears. "All right, mousie pie. *You can help*," I said. I patted the top of his tiny head. You see, Benjamin is my favorite nephew!

Benjamin is my favorite nephew!

THE TELLTAIL TAVERN

Trap began his story. "Do you remember that friend of mine I used to play pool with?" he asked. "The one with the scar on his tail and a black patch on one eye? His name is Lefty Limburger. Last Sunday I was playing pool with Lefty at the Telltail Tavern. Have you ever been there?"

I frowned. "I'd rather eat a piece of moldy cheese than be seen in that place!"

"You don't know what you're missing," Trap said. "Each night, there's something exciting going on. Yesterday there was a wrestling match between a karate black belt and a pool champion. **You should have seen it!** The black belt's paws were flying, but then the pool champ started

Each night, there's something exciting going on.

slapping him with slices of **Swiss cheese**. . . .”

“Get to the point!” Thea snapped.

“Well, I met up with my old friend Lefty. And he told me a secret,” Trap began. He lowered his voice. “You see, his niece is a friend of the mailmouse’s cousin. And she lives next to the brother-in-law of one of the guards at the mouseum. Well, he told the brother-in-law, who told the mailmouse’s cousin, who told Lefty’s niece, who told Lefty.”

“Who told who *what*?” I asked, growing IMPATIENT.

“Don’t get your tail in a twist, Gerry,” said Trap, smirking. “That’s what I’m about to tell you. The mouseum guard said that the *Mona Mousa* has been taken to a lab to be **X-RAYED**. And that can only mean one thing. There is something hidden underneath the painting!”

Thea Has a New Boyfriend . . . Again!

Now it was Thea's turn. She smoothed her fur and began her story.

"Do you remember my boyfriend?" she asked. "The one with the **blue eyes** and blond fur? He always wears cheddar *cologne*. . . ."

"You mean the one who lives in a castle and is allergic to blue cheese?" I asked.

"No, no," my sister snapped. "I got rid of that one ages ago."

I tried again. "Is it the one who owns a cheese factory?"

"No, no," Thea said impatiently. "He's ancient history. We broke up six months ago."

"I give up," I said. Thea has had so many

boyfriends, I would need six extra paws to count them all!

"Well, now I have a *new* boyfriend," Thea said. "His name is Frick Tapioca, and he is the mouseum's art expert. He told me a secret. While they were restoring the *Mona Mousa,* Frick discovered that there is another painting underneath the surface. He is examining the **X-RAY** results right now!"

Nine Minutes Flat

Minutes later, we all bundled into Thea's yellow sports car. We reached the mouseum in nine minutes flat.

"Only nine minutes from the office to the mouseum," Thea said proudly. "That's my new record!"

I was shaking like a mouse who's been cornered by a hungry cat. I used to think horror movies were scary. But Thea's driving was even scarier!

"Holey cheese! I'm going to have a heart attack, I know it!" I squeaked. "You should never run a **RED** light like that, you know. That truck was so close, I was sure it would chop off my tail!"

Trap, of course, was impressed. "Not bad,

Cousin," he told Thea. "Although I'm sure I could have done better. I bet I could have made it in eight and a half minutes!"

Thea revved up the engine. "Oh, yeah? I accept your challenge! Let's do it again!"

"Oh, no, you don't! **LET ME OUT!**" I cried. I leaped out of the car. My legs felt like jelly.

"**I know one thing for sure**," I mumbled. "**I will never get in a car with you mice again.** I'm too fond of my fur!"

IF THE *MONA MOUSA* COULD SQUEAK

The mouseum was ENORMOUSE. The ground floor housed ancient relics, like MUMMIES from Egypt and fragments of old cheese pots. The second floor held displays of paintings by the *old masters*, like Botticheddar and Jan van Edam.

The gallery of modern art was on the third floor. I recently visited there to see the famouse painting of cans of cheese soup by the modern artist Ratty Mousehol. I'm not sure if I liked it, but it

The mouseum was enormouse. . . .

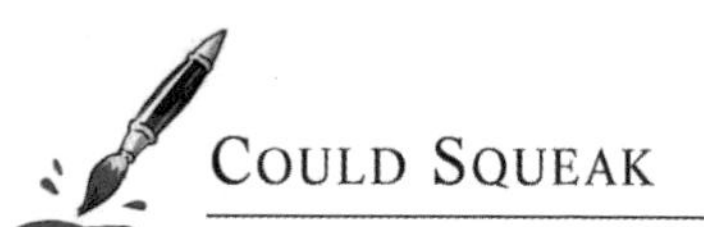

did make me hungry!

As we climbed the marble staircase to the second floor, I told Benjamin the story of the *Mona Mousa*. The portrait was painted in 1504 by the great painter and scientist Mousardo da Munchie.

"The *Mona Mousa*'s smile is very mysterious," I explained. "It's almost as if she knows a secret."

"I wonder what the *Mona Mousa* would say if she could squeak," Benjamin said. "Maybe she is smiling because she knows about the hidden painting."

We climbed to the next floor. The gallery of modern art

was all chrome-plated steel and glass.

"We won't be on this floor for long," Thea teased. "I know you don't like art unless it's **older** than one of Grandfather William's whiskers."

Just then, a mouse dressed all in **black** approached us. He wore a pair of round glasses perched on top of his snout. It was the famous art critic Arty Fartsyfur. I disliked him on sight.

"DAAAHRRR-LING!" he shouted, running toward Thea.

"DAAAHRRR-LING!" she replied. The two of them kissed each other on both cheeks.

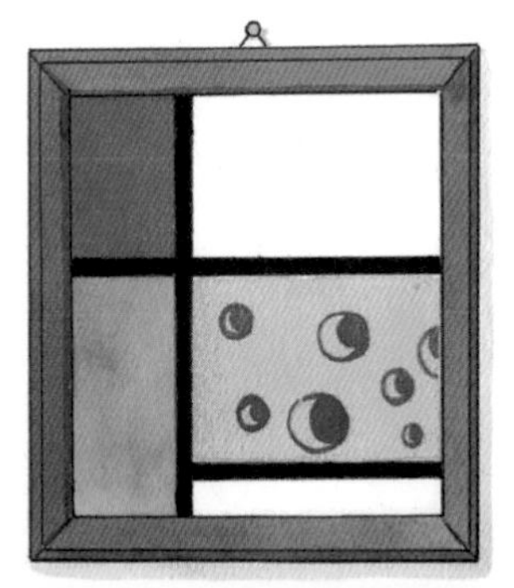

"What a PHONY," grumbled Trap with his mouth full. He had already found the snack bar and was munching on a frozen cheesesicle. "We're here to work, not to chat!"

"Good-bye, daaahrling!" Thea waved to Arty. Then she led us up one more flight of stairs, to the fourth floor. That's where the mouseum's offices and lab were.

When we got to the lab, we were greeted by a very *shy* yet **charming** mouse. It was Frick Tapioca, my sister's current boyfriend.

Frick looked **startled**. "Th-Th-Thea!" he stammered. "I didn't expect to see you!"

"How is the research on the painting coming along?" Thea asked.

Frick frowned. "I can't squeak

Frick Tapioca

about it. That's TOP-SECRET INFORMATION!"

Thea stroked Frick's ear. "There are no secrets between us, are there, my little niblet?" she crooned.

Frick's fur went red. "What would you like to know?"

"Everything! **Now!**" Thea demanded.

"*Well …*" Frick hesitated. Then he looked over at Trap, Benjamin, and me. "Who are these people?"

Thea's voice turned sugary again. "They're family. You can trust them," she said.

"Last week, I started to restore the *Mona Mousa,*" Frick whispered. "I scratched a fragment of paint off the canvas and realized there was another painting underneath! I had the painting X-RAYED. My hunch was right. Mousardo da Munchie created a hidden

painting underneath the *Mona Mousa*!"

Frick produced a CD from under his white lab coat. "The hidden painting shows eleven objects," he said. "I used a computer to reconstruct them. They're all on this disk."

Thea quickly grabbed the CD from him. "Thank you, my sweet," she said. "I'll just borrow this for a little while. You'll get it back the next time we see each other."

Frick beamed. "I'll see you again soon, then? When?" He cleared his throat. "Uh, how about tonight?"

Thea stroked Frick's ear again. "I'm busy tonight, my sweet. But maybe next week. Or the week after that."

Simeon Starchfur

Just then, the mouseum's curator, Simeon Starchfur, came by. He was a tall, lean, distinguished-looking mouse. He wore a blue bow tie and a red vest, complete with a gold watch and chain.

Starchfur kissed my sister's paw. "Good day to you, *Miss Stilton*. What brings you here?" he inquired politely.

"Good morning. What a pleasure to see you again," Thea **squeaked**. "Please forgive me, but I must run. Good-bye!"

We followed Thea down the stairs and back to the street. Then everyone followed her into her *sports car*. Everyone but me, that is. I decided to take a taxi. I'm too fond of my fur!

THEA'S MIRROR

When we got back to the office, we locked ourselves in. We had a lot of work to do.

"Since we'll be working on this all night," Trap grumbled, "I'd better order some food!"

Trap picked up the phone. "Give me your MEGA-HUGE PIZZA," I heard him say. "No, make that a super-deluxe mega-huge pizza. Make it extra spicy. And bill it to my cousin Geronimo."

I sighed. I hate spicy food. But I didn't feel like arguing with Trap. We had a lot of work to do.

"I can help, Uncle," Benjamin said. He sat

down at the computer and inserted the CD.

Images appeared on the screen. Frick had taken the X RAY of the hidden picture and colored it in with a computer. We could make out eleven mysterious objects. There was a statue, a fountain, and a crown. But the rest of the items were hard to identify.

Then I noticed tiny writing on the bottom of the screen.

"What's that?" I asked, pointing. Benjamin enlarged the words so we could read them.

ELEVEN PLACES ARE YOURS TO FIND
ELEVEN LETTERS YOU MUST COMBINE
ONE SINGLE WORD WILL GIVE YOU THE KEY
TO SOLVE THE MYSTERY I GIVE TO THEE

The writing didn't make any sense! It looked like some kind of **lost language**.

Then Thea's eyes lit up. "I think I've got it," she said. She took a mirror out of her purse and placed it in front of the writing. As if by magic, the words suddenly became clear.

ELEVEN PLACES ARE YOURS TO FIND
ELEVEN LETTERS YOU MUST COMBINE
ONE SINGLE WORD WILL GIVE YOU THE KEY
TO SOLVE THE MYSTERY I GIVE TO THEE

"I know, Uncle!" Benjamin said, his voice filled with excitement. "The eleven pictures must represent eleven places in New Mouse City. There must be a letter *hidden* in each place. We just have to visit each of the places to solve the mystery."

"By cheese, I think he's got it!" I exclaimed. "What do you think, Trap?"

But Trap wasn't paying attention. He was munching on the super-deluxe MEGA-HUGE PIZZA and watching cartoons on the TV in my office.

"You could give us a paw, you know," Thea scolded. "Why should you get equal profits if you don't do equal work?"

But Trap didn't budge. "**You take care** of the brainy end of this operation, and **I'll take care** of the business end," he said.

So, without Trap's help, we worked through the night. We leafed through *old books* about the history of Mouse Island. We examined map after map. Finally, we were able to identify all eleven places. . . .

The Pelican's Pillar
(at the fish market)

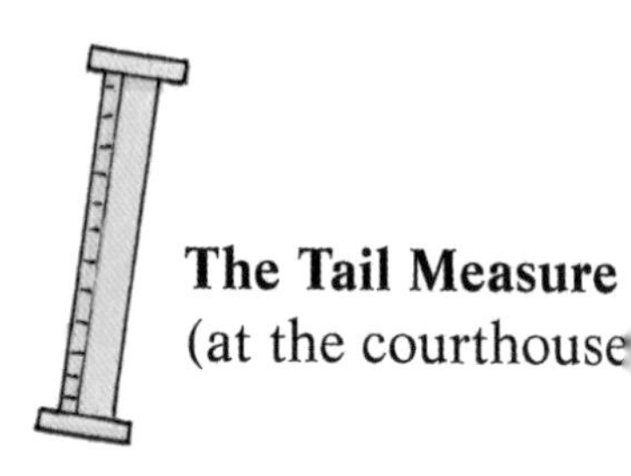

The Tail Measure
(at the courthouse

The Seal of Mouselius
(at the cheese factory)

The Goblet of the Silver Rodent (at the mouseum)

The Fountain of Cheddar
(at the cheese factory)

The Cat's Rock
(at the amousement park)

The Arched Ceiling
(at the Tricks for Tails joke shop)

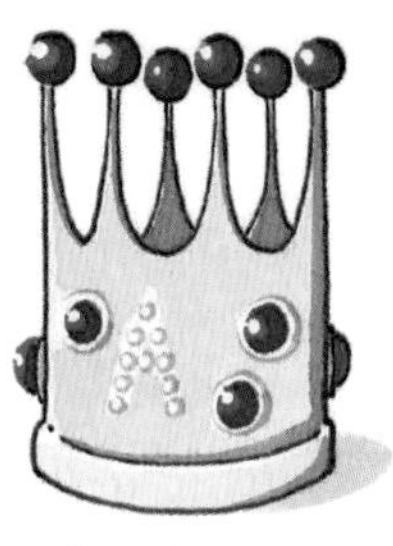

The Crown of Princess Angorat Curlyfur VII
(at the bank)

The Pools at the Ancient Baths
(at the Rats La Lanne Gym)

The Statue of Emeritus Fellowmouse
(at the elementary school)

The Sundial
(at the Telltail Tavern)

ELEVEN PLACES ARE YOURS TO FIND
ELEVEN LETTERS YOU MUST COMBINE
ONE SINGLE WORD WILL GIVE YOU THE KEY
TO SOLVE THE MYSTERY I GIVE TO THEE

THE PELICAN'S PILLAR

"This won't be easy," I said. "We need to visit each of the eleven places and search for a letter hidden in each one to solve the mystery. That's like searching for a needle in a stack of STRING CHEESE!"

Trap smiled confidently. "Don't get your fur in a tangle, Cousinkins." he said. "I've got friends **all over town**. You name it, and I'll tell you how to find it."

"All right, then. How about the Pelican's Pillar?" I asked. "It's somewhere in the fish market — but where?"

"No problem," Trap said. "**I'm** a legend at the fish market. **I'm** famouse as a great shark hunter."

I rolled my eyes. From the way my cousin

talks, you'd think he'd captured **JAWS**!

"Go to the squid stall and ask for Coral Cockle," Trap continued. "Tell her Trap sent you. She'll take you where you need to go."

Thea and I headed to the fish market together. As we approached, we heard the loud **SQUEAKS** of fish sellers. The market was packed with stalls of fishermice selling seafood.

I had never seen so many fish in one place. There were tuna and flounder. Crabs and lobsters. Clams and oysters. Even squids and sharks!

I began to feel nervous. The fish seemed to be glaring at me with their creepy bulging eyes. I was so anxious that I didn't notice a nearby fish seller about to dump a bucket of seawater over his fish to keep them fresh. All of a sudden . . . SPLASH! The salty water drenched me.

"Jumping gerbil babies!" I cried. My suit was RUINED!

Thea shook her head. "**You should be more careful**," she scolded.

"It wasn't my fault," I protested. I stepped toward Thea . . .

. . . and slipped on a fish bone! I fell flat on my back, knocking into a fish stall.

A giant tuna fish plopped into my arms.

"Should I wrap that up for you?" the fish seller asked.

"WH-WH-WHAT? NO WAY!" I said.

By now, a crowd had gathered. They seemed to think my fish problems were funny.

"Everyone's staring at us," Thea whispered. "Oh, Gerry Berry, why do you always have to make a scene?"

"I told you, it's not my fault!" I cried. I stood up . . .

. . . and backed right into an octopus! Its slimy tentacles wrapped around my neck.

"I GIVE UP!" I squeaked.

That Mouse Is Something Else!

A female fish seller stormed up to me. "Paws off my octopus!" she shouted angrily.

I pushed the tentacles off me, shuddering.

"You must be Coral Cockle!" Thea said, smiling. "Don't pay any attention to my brother. He's a terrible klutz."

I couldn't take it anymore. "But it was her slimy octopus that —"

Thea jabbed me in the ribs. "We need her help," she whispered to me. Then she turned back to Coral.

"Our cousin Trap said you could help us," Thea said.

Coral's face lit up. "Why didn't you say so?

That mouse is something else! Sharper than a block of aged cheddar."

"*We hear he's quite good with sharks, too,*" I said, hoping to find out the truth behind Trap's tall tales.

"Sharks? You mean anchovies, don't you?" she giggled. "Unless you don't know the difference between a shark and an anchovy."

"Of course I —" I began indignantly, but Thea jabbed me in the ribs again.

Coral reached into her pocket and took out a **greasy** picture. It showed Trap holding a trophy.

"Trap is the anchovy-eating champion," she said dreamily.

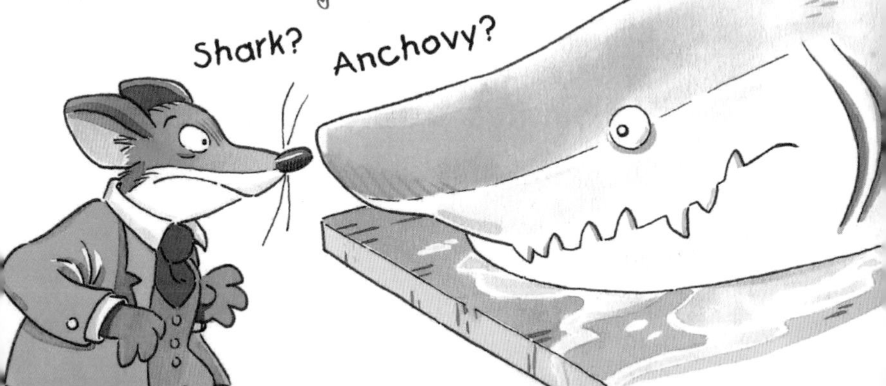

"Three hundred fifty-three in one minute. Amazing!"

"That's our cousin," Thea said. "He told us we should see the Pelican's Pillar on our visit. Can you take us to it?"

Coral nodded. She led us through the stalls to a tall marble column near the water's edge. We could see carvings of pelicans on top of the column. Each bird held a fish in its beak.

We examined the column carefully. Was there a letter hidden there somewhere?

Then I saw it. One of the fish tails was different than the others. It was clearly shaped like the letter "Y."

"Do you see it?" I whispered to Thea.

My sister nodded.

"You know, it's strange," Coral remarked. "A little old lady came by around six o'clock this morning. She asked to see the Pelican's Pillar, too."

Thea raised an eyebrow. "What did she look like?" she asked. She took out a pen and paper and began taking notes.

Coral tried to remember. "She wore a red head scarf with blue dots. She carried a basketful of apples. We made a trade: an octopus for an apple," she said. She took an *apple* out of her pocket and bit into it.

Coral Cockle

We said good-bye to Coral.

"Tell Trap to come and visit sometime," she called after us.

Back at the office, Thea drew a picture of the old lady. Very strange, I thought. I was glad that we had solved the first clue of the *Mona Mousa* mystery.

But who was this elderly mouse? Was she trying to crack the code, too?

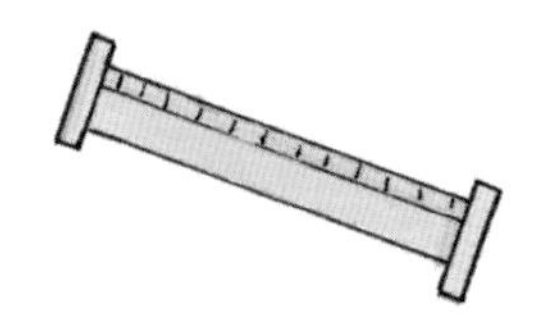

The Tail Measure

We went to work on the second clue: the *Tail Measure*.

I knew the Tail Measure was a kind of ancient yardstick. It was used in the year 1000 B.C. (Before Cats). I also knew that it was kept at the courthouse. But how would we find it?

"It'll be as easy as cheese pie!" Trap said smugly. "Go see my friend Larry Licorice at the courthouse. Tell him I sent you."

I had a lot of work to catch up on at the office. So Thea went down to the courthouse on her own. Then she sent me this fax.

URGENT: FAX
TO: The Stilton Publishing Company
ATTENTION: Geronimo Stilton

Dearest Gerry,

Larry Licorice is a sticky character. At first, he asked me to pay him a hefty sum to get the information I needed. When I mentioned Trap's name, though, he said he would help me for free. He said he owed Trap a favor, and now they could call it even.

Larry took me to the court's archives, where the Tail Measure is kept. It has no engraved letters on it. But as I examined it, I realized that the Tail Measure is shaped like the letter I.

See you tomorrow,

Thea

P.S. Yesterday, a widow wearing a veil asked if she could take a picture of the Tail Measure.

The Goblet of the Silver Rodent

The next day, we looked for the third clue: the Goblet of the **Silver Rodent**.

Thea and I went back to the mouseum to examine it. But the display cabinet was empty, except for this note:

The Goblet of the Silver Rodent

ca 1000 B.C.

On loan to the famouse film director

Steven Spielmouse

We returned to the office. Trap was busy playing video games and **slurping** a bowl of cheese soup.

"Trap, it's still morning. What are you doing eating soup?" I asked.

Trap crumbled crackers into his bowl. "It's my after-breakfast snack," he said.

Cracker crumbs tumbled all over my nice clean desk. "Would you mind eating somewhere else?" I asked, annoyed.

Trap shrugged and turned off the game. As he stood up, he knocked over his bowl of BOILING-HOT soup. It spilled all over my desk!

"**SLIMY SWISS ROLLS! MY PAPERS!**" I shrieked.

Do you think Trap stopped to clean up the mess? Of course not. He went to get a fresh bowl. But Thea stopped him.

"Trap, do you know the film director Steven Spielmouse?" she asked.

"Of course I do," Trap answered. Then he frowned. "Although I strongly advise you not to mention my name. If he finds out that we are related, deny everything!"

I had no idea what Trap might have done to upset the great director. But we had to try to find the clue anyway. Thea and I rushed to the film studio.

The film set was covered with sand and fake palm trees. We saw Steven Spielmouse squeaking orders into a bullhorn.

"Who is the cheddarface who turned on the SNOW machine?" he yelled angrily. "Can't you see this movie takes place in a desert? A DESERT!"

"What a loudmouse," I remarked to Thea. But my sister had spotted something.

"I think I see the silver goblet," she whispered, pointing.

To the side of the set was a small room with glass windows — the film director's office. Inside we could see a mouse dressed like a Roman gladiator. The mouse was inspecting the goblet. Then he set it down and sneaked out of the office.

How strange! I thought. Who else could be looking for the silver goblet?

As quiet as churchmice, Thea and I sneaked in. Thea picked up the goblet. Then we heard an angry voice behind us.

"**Paws off** that cup!"

It was Steven Spielmouse!

"Who are you, anyway?" the director demanded.

"My name is Stilton, Geronimo Stilton. This is my sister, Thea," I blurted out.

Thea stepped on my tail, but she was too late. I had forgotten Trap's warning.

Spielmouse frowned. "*Stilton? Stilton?* Are you related to a mouse named Trap?"

"Um, he's a distant relative," I stammered. "*Very* distant."

"I've been trying to track down that rat for two years!" the director shrieked. "When I was filming *Ship of Mice,* he drove a speedboat into the ship right before I had to shoot the scene. The ship sank! You can't have a movie called *Ship of Mice* without a ship!"

Spielmouse stomped around his office. "If I ever get my paws on Trap Stilton . . ."

While the director fumed, Thea and I slowly backed out of the office. Then we scampered out of the studio as quickly as we could.

"Don't worry, Gerry Berry," Thea said, ***giggling***. "I saw a letter engraved on the cup. It's an **H**!"

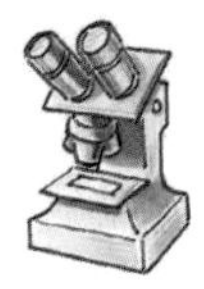

THE SEAL AND THE FOUNTAIN

Back at the office, I found Trap sitting at **my** desk. He had cleaned up the soup. But now he was dipping sugar cubes into a jar of honey.

"Trap, **how can you eat that?**" I asked, horrified.

"It's my *after*-after-breakfast snack," he replied. "Want some?"

"No, thanks," I answered disdainfully. "By the way, we found out that you are much in demand in the movie business. Steven Spielmouse can't wait to get his paws on you!"

Trap smirked. "Ah, yes, the *Ship of Mice* **incident**," he said. "It wasn't my fault,

really. That big ship of his got in my way. Oh, I lined up the next two clues for you. They are both at the CHEESE FACTORY. Ask to see Benny Bluewhiskers, and tell him I sent you."

Thea, Benjamin, and I headed out right away. Thea took Benjamin in her sports car. As for me, I took the bus. I'm too fond of my fur to drive with that **MADMOUSE**!

We met at the Cheese Factory. It's a big building where all of the cheese on Mouse Island is produced. Each one is INSPECTED, *measured*, and SEALED before it is sold in stores.

We had to find two clues at the factory. The fourth clue, the Seal of Mouselius, once belonged to the legendary mouse who invented cheese. The fifth clue, the Cheddar Fountain, flowed in the courtyard.

When we entered, a **plump** mouse wearing a white coat came to greet us.

"*Welcome!* I am Benny Bluewhiskers," he said. "Your cousin Trap told me you were coming. Let me show you the lab!"

He led us into an enormouse room. It was stacked with piles of different cheeses. Mice wearing white overalls scurried about, MEASURING and *inspecting* the cheese.

A mouse ran up to Benny. "Sir, we are about to send off a load of cheddar."

Benny looked **SERIOUS**. "This needs immediate attention," he said. He led us to a table stacked with blocks of cheese.

The mouse handed Benny a certificate. Benny examined it carefully. "**Cheddar**, eh?" he asked. Then he measured one of the cheese blocks from end to end with a brass ruler.

"Excellent," he said. "Now to check the

Benny Bluewhiskers

cheese's maturity."

Next Benny stuck a long wooden stick into the cheese. He **sniffed** it delicately.

"Matured to perfection!" he announced.

Then he produced a **color chart**. He held it up to the cheese.

"Amber yellow," he said. "Just right."

Finally, Benny took a pen and a seal from his pocket. He signed the certificate, then stamped it with the **SEAL**.

Benny turned back to us. "By the way, how is Trap? He used to work here as a taster, you know. I remember he wanted to create the world's **BIGGEST WHEEL** of cheese!"

"I'm sorry, Benny," Thea said. "But we're in

a hurry. Could we see the Seal of Mouselius and the Fountain of Cheddar now?"

"Of course!" Benny said. He scurried away from the cheddar and led us to the mouseum inside the factory. There, displayed in a glass case, was the Seal of Mouselius. It looked a bit like Benny's seal, only much older. The bottom of the silver seal was engraved with the letter T.

Then Benny took us to the courtyard, which held a round marble fountain. In the center of the fountain was a statue of the Muse of Cheese. Melted cheddar SPURTED from her cornucopia.

Thea took pictures with

her camera while Benjamin and I inspected the fountain. I didn't find any trace of a letter. But then Benjamin pointed to the decoration around the rim of the pool.

"They look like lots of **B**'s in a row," he pointed out. Benjamin is so clever!

On the bus ride home, I wrote in my notebook:

Tomorrow I will go to the amousement park in search of the next letter.

P.S. Benny told us that he noticed a mouse at the factory wearing a pair of pants with flowers all over them. In the afternoon, another mouse wearing a red-and-white-striped vest showed up. They were both interested in our clues. . . .

THE CAT'S ROCK

The next day, Benjamin and I set out in search of the sixth clue.

Trap, of course, had a contact for us at the AMOUSEMENT PARK. "Ask to see my friend **Chuck Choptail**. His friends call him **SLICK**. He is the owner of the **roller coaster**," Trap had told us.

We arrived at the amousement park at six o'clock. The sun was setting, and the bright lights of the rides were starting to come on. We could see the big Ferris wheel, the merry-go-round, and the bumper cars.

I began to feel nervous. Scary movies horrify me. Thea's driving makes me weak in the knees. But the fast rides at an amousement park *really* terrify me.

Benjamin, however, was VERY EXCITED. "Can we please go on the merry-go-round, Uncle Geronimo? And then get popcorn? And then can we play Whack-a-Cat?"

I smiled. It is hard to say no to my nephew. "Let's find the clue first," I said.

We walked over to the roller coaster. A short mouse was sitting on a barrel of fish, counting a pile of coins. When he saw us, he muttered, "One adult and one child?"

"Mr. Chuck Choptail?" I asked.

Chuck Choptail

"We need some information. My cousin Trap said you might help us."

The little mouse broke into a big smile. "Good old Trap! Are you really his cousin? You don't look like him at all. You're so skinny!"

"He's my cousin, all right," I replied. "Anyway, he told us about a cat-shaped rock here at the amousement park. Can you take us to see it?"

"Anything for a cousin of Trap's," Slick replied. "But first, how about a nice ride on the **roller coaster**?"

I gulped. "Oh, no, thank you," I said.

But Benjamin tugged on my sleeve. "Please, Uncle. It looks like fun!"

I hated to disappoint my nephew. "You can take a ride on it if you want."

SLICK frowned. "You can't let a little mouse like that go on by himself!" he scolded. He pushed us both toward a red roller coaster car. Benjamin hopped right inside. I started to back away, but Slick tripped me with his paw.

"Fasten your seat belts and enjoy the ride," Slick said, grinning.

"Let me out!" I screamed. But it was too late. The car

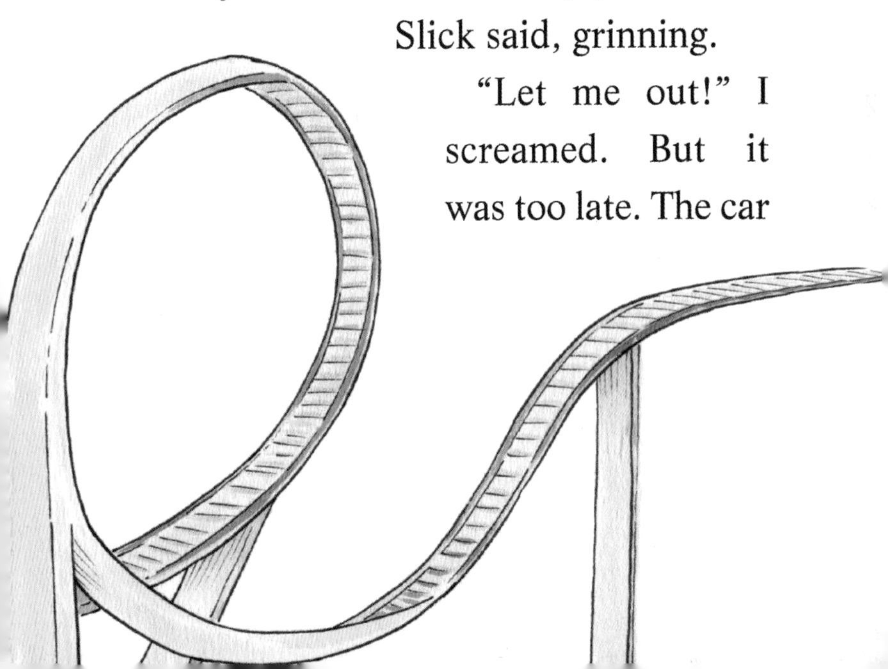

had started lurching forward. I was trapped!

I closed my eyes and clutched the bar in front of me. My paws were sweaty with **FRIGHT**. I could feel the car climbing up the steep track.

"Uncle, look how **HIGH** we are!" Benjamin called out happily.

I couldn't bear to open my eyes. But it didn't matter. Even though I couldn't *see* what was happening, I could feel it.

Zoom! The car plunged down a hill. We curved sharply to the **left**. Then to the **right**. The car made an upside-down loop. So did my stomach. Then another loop, and another one. My insides turned over and over.

Then we did it all again — **BACKWARD**!

Benjamin shrieked with delight. But I was **TOO SCARED** to even scream.

After what seemed like hours, the car

finally stopped. I opened my eyes. Slick came running toward us.

"I know any cousin of Trap's must be a roller coaster fanatic," he said. "Want to go again?"

"**NO**," I squeaked weakly. There was no way I was falling for another one of Slick's cruel tricks. I staggered out of the car and collapsed against a nearby rock. I felt like a slice of cheese that had been left out in the sun too long.

Then everything went black.

When I woke up, Benjamin was fanning me with a newspaper.

"Uncle, are you all right?" he asked.

Slick was gently slapping my face. "Are you *sure* you're

related to Trap Stilton?"

I wanted to get far away from the amousement park — fast. "Where is the Cat's Rock?" I asked weakly.

Slick smirked. "Right under your tail!" he said.

I struggled to my feet. My head was still spinning. Even so, I could see that the rock I had fainted on was shaped like a cat. The letter **R** was engraved in the stone.

My head was still spinning.

Through my stupor, I could hear Slick talking to Benjamin.

"That's funny," he was saying. "Just yesterday, a mouse wearing a clown costume asked me to show him the CAT'S ROCK!"

TRICKS FOR TAILS

The next morning, I found Trap sitting at my desk *again*. This time he was munching on cheese-flavored popcorn.

"Let me guess," I said. "Is that your *after*-after-after breakfast snack?"

"No, it's my after-after-breakfast pre-lunch snack," Trap replied. He grinned. "I got a call from Slick. He told me you have a weak stomach. I hope you didn't ruin my good reputation."

"GOOD REPUTATION, MY PAW," I muttered. "Where do I go to find the seventh clue — the Arched Ceiling?"

"Head to the Tricks for Tails joke shop in Fastrat Lane," Trap said. "I work there sometimes, so the owner is a friend of mine."

This time I went alone. I headed to Fastrat Lane and found the store, just as Trap had said. I pushed open the glass door and stepped inside. And then . . . a huge cat leaped on my head!

"Putrid cheese puffs!" I screamed, terrified.

A plump mouse wearing red-and-blue-striped pants walked up to me, chortling. He took the cat off my head.

"It's stuffed, see?" he said. "I just love that trick."

The mouse put down the cat and held out his paw. "Paws Prankster, owner of Tricks for Tails," he said. "Have a seat."

Paws pointed to a stool with a red pillow on it. I sat down gratefully.

Snap! A mousetrap hidden in the cushion pinched my tail.

"Cheese niblets!" I shrieked, leaping up.

Paws laughed. "Sorry," he said. "You look rather pale. Maybe a nice morsel of cheese would help."

He handed me a piece of cheese, and I took a bite . . .

. . . and spit it right out. It was rubber!

Paws clutched his belly. He was laughing so hard, he was crying. "I love customers like you. You fall for it every time," he

said, wiping away his tears. "How can I help you? We have quite a selection. Maybe you'd like a nice stinky cheese bomb? Or a cat in a can? Or how about a surprise sugar cube? As it melts in your cup, it reveals a rubber worm!"

He wiggled the **WORM** in front of my face.

"No, thanks," I replied. "I'm here because —"

"Look out!" Paws screamed, pointing to my jacket. "There's a rattlesnake on your shoulder!"

I looked at my shoulder — and saw a snake! I jumped, screaming. The snake fell to the floor. That's when I noticed it was only rubber.

Paws began slapping his knees. "Hee-hee-hee!" he howled. "You aren't an actor, are you? Nobody could *really* be such a CHEESEBRAIN!"

I had had enough. I started to storm out—but the rug slipped out from underneath my paws, and I went flying! The next thing I knew, I was rolled up inside it!

"I can't take any more," I wailed. "My cousin Trap sent me. I need some information."

"Why didn't you say so?" Paws asked. "Trap is one of my best friends. He always tells me the funniest stories. He has this ridiculous cousin named Geronimo Stilton. . . ."

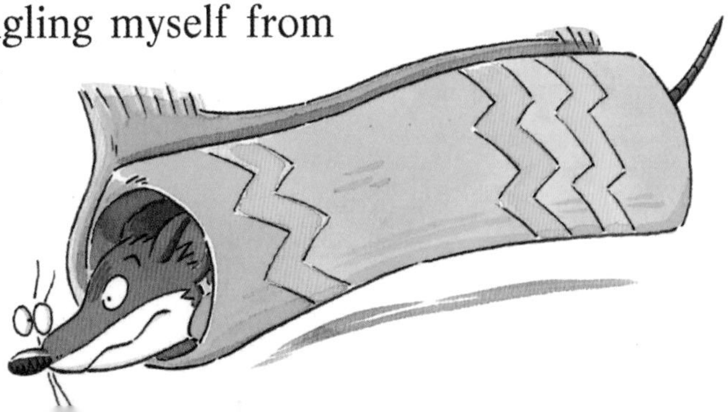

"That's me, I am *Geronimo Stilton!*" I cried, untangling myself from the rug. "I would like to see the ceiling in your cellar. Will you please help?"

Paws shook his head. "Why is everyone so interested in my cellar all of a sudden?" he ***wondered*** out loud. "Just yesterday, a cute mouse dressed up like **Little Red Riding Hood** came to see it."

I sighed. Someone had beaten me to the clue again!

Paws opened a small door leading to a narrow, dimly lit spiral staircase. I went down slowly, checking each step to make sure there were no booby traps. I didn't think my heart could take any more tricks!

When I got to the cellar, I looked up at the old, arched ceiling. The letter **L** was carved right in the center!

First-class Home

That night, we all went to Trap's house. Thea drove Trap and Benjamin. As for me, I took the bus again. *I'm too fond of my fur!*

My cousin's house was once a train. The walls are covered in wood paneling. It has a big kitchen in front of the first-class car. Trap converted it into his living room. The room is filled with red velvet stuffed armchairs. They are so comfortable! When you sit in them, you feel like you're settling in for a nice, cozy ride on the rails.

Trap converted the boxcar into his bedroom. When he pushes on a spring, his bed flips down from the wall. It's very UNUSUAL — but then again, so is Trap.

"Coffee, anyone?" Trap asked. He is very

proud of his shiny brass coffee machine. There is a winged rodent on top.

Trap started up the machine. Steam puffed out of the jets. Soon he poured us PIPING HOT coffee into small cups. They were marked with the initials M.I.R.: Mouse Island Railway.

I curled up in a leather armchair in front of the fireplace, where bright flames crackled merrily. Benjamin curled up in my lap and fell asleep. Outside, cold winds were blowing, but we all felt WARM AND TOASTY in Trap's first-class home.

Thea struck her cup with her spoon to get our attention.

"Today I went to Rodent Bank, where the crown of Princess Angorat Curlyfur VII is

My cousin's house was once a train.

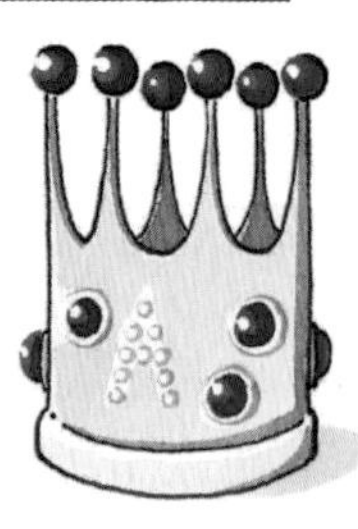

kept," she said. "As you know, it is our eighth clue. I discovered that in the middle of the crown there is an **A** made of tiny diamonds."

"That makes eight letters," Benjamin said sleepily. "Only three more to go!"

"There is something else," Thea said, and her tone was serious. "As I was leaving, I saw a strange mouse wearing a raincoat. He was watching me from behind his newspaper. This can't be a coincidence. He must belong to a family of mice, just like us, who are trying to solve the mystery of the *Mona Mousa*!"

EMERITUS FELLOWMOUSE

We had no time to lose. If we wanted to break the story of the secret behind the *Mona Mousa,* we would have to find all the clues before those other mysterious mice did.

The ninth clue was a statue of Emeritus Fellowmouse, the founder of the first elementary school in New Mouse City.

"Go to see my old teacher, *Abacus Fastsums,*" Trap suggested. "He can tell you all about it."

So Benjamin and I headed out early the next morning. We got to the school at seven o'clock, before classes started.

Abacus Fastsums, an old mouse with **gray** fur, was perched behind his desk. He wore

thick glasses and was SCRIBBLING into a notebook.

"What can I do for you?" he asked wearily. Then he saw Benjamin. "Is this your son?"

"Actually —" I began. But he interrupted me.

"I assume you are here to enroll him," Abacus said.

"No, I —"

"Well, you can't! It's too late! The enrollment list is closed," Abacus informed me.

"You don't understand —"

"What? Speak up!" the old mouse shouted. "I'm a bit hard of hearing."

I raised my voice. "I've been sent by Trap, an old student of yours."

"What? Hours? I think it's seven o'clock," Abacus replied.

I tried again. "Trap told me about the statue of Emeritus Fellowmouse."

Abacus frowned. "WHAT? Farmhouse? This is a school, not a farmhouse."

"No, the **statue** of Emeritus Fellowmouse!" I repeated impatiently. I pointed out the window, where the statue could be seen in the courtyard.

Abacus nodded. "Oh, the statue. Yesterday a mouse came in, a rather **MATURE** student. He wanted to get a close look at it. Who did you say sent you?"

"TRAP!" I shouted.

He finally caught on. "What? Trap? Why didn't you say so? I'll never forget Trap. He was the most TROUBLESOME student I ever had," Abacus said. "Once, he climbed on top of the statue of Emeritus Fellowmouse to put a banana on his snout. Then there was the time he NAILED SHUT THE DRAWERS on my desk. And the day he put chewing gum on my chair. What a pest! And yet . . ."

The old mouse looked moved. He wiped a tear away from his eye. "Trap is the only one who still sends me Christmas cards. Look here!"

He opened a desk drawer and took out a big bundle of cards tied with red ribbon. I recognized my cousin's writing. *Abacus* put away the cards and walked toward the door.

"Follow me!" he said.

He led us to the statue. I examined it carefully. Emeritus Fellowmouse stood on a school desk. He held up an inkwell engraved with the letter **S**.

I turned to Abacus. "Thank you for your time," I said. "I hope it wasn't too much trouble."

"Bubbles? I don't see any bubbles," Abacus said.

Benjamin *giggled*. I just sighed and waved good-bye.

The Pools at the Ancient Baths

Only two more places to check out! Number ten, the Pools of the Ancient Baths, could be found at the Rats La Lanne Gym.

Jock Musclemouse

Trap told me to talk to his friend JOCK MUSCLEMOUSE, a personal trainer who worked there.

When I got to the gym, I was greeted by a rat the size of a cheese delivery truck. He had more muscles than a hunk of Swiss cheese has holes!

The mouse picked me up under one arm. "You must be here for the full treatment," he said.

"Well, actually, I —" I began.

Jock dropped me in the changing room. "Put on some sweats," he instructed me.

I changed into sweatpants and a T-shirt. When I came out, Jock PUSHED me through a door and shut it behind me.

"Is this the way to the pools?" I asked.

Then I saw that Jock had put me in a closet — a very *hot* closet. I was in a sauna! I looked at the thermometer on the wall.

"Holey cheese!" I cried. "It's a HUNDRED DEGREES in here!"

I pushed open the door, gasping for air. Jock looked surprised. "Done already?"

Jock turned on a faucet on the wall, and cold water splashed all over me.

"You don't understand," I said. "I'm here for —"

Jock picked me up again. This time, he dropped me on a treadmill! It was moving

at maximum speed.

"Jumping gerbil babies!" I panted. "How do you stop this thing?"

Jock switched off the treadmill. Then he plopped me on a table. "Nothing like a good massage to soothe your tired muscles," he said. "It's all included in the price."

Jock began to knead my muscles with his powerful paws. I felt like a slice of cheese going through a shredder.

"Eeeenough!" I screamed. I JUMPED OFF the massage table and ran to the door.

Jock grabbed me by the tail. "Are you planning to run off without paying?" he asked. Then he slapped a bill in my paw. I couldn't believe the amount.

"I didn't ask for a sauna! Or a shower! Or a massage!" I squeaked. "I ABSOLUTELY refuse to pay!"

"How do you stop this thing?"

Just then, Thea came by, wearing a trendy workout outfit.

"Geronimo? What are you doing here?"

Jock SCOWLED. "Do you know this guy? He was trying to scurry away without paying!"

"This is the most exclusive gym in New Mouse City," Thea HISSED in my ear. "You're making me look bad! So pay up now!"

I *wrote out* a check, furious, while Jock glared at me.

As I stormed off, Thea stopped me. "**What brings you here, anyway?**" she asked.

"I'm looking for the tenth letter," I explained.

"You didn't have to come all this way," Thea said. "I looked at the pools this morning. They're shaped like the letter **N**."

THE LAST LETTER

After I gave Jock a **mega-huge** check, he became a lot friendlier. He told me a mouse in baseball gear had visited the gym, looking for the pools.

Thea, Trap, Benjamin, and I held an emergency meeting in my office.

"Those mysterious mice may have already solved the mystery!" I said. "We need to run to the sundial at the Telltail Tavern to find the eleventh letter. ***ANY VOLUNTEERS?***"

Trap smirked. "The letter on the sundial is **U**, ratlets," he announced. "I was at the Telltail yesterday. I wanted to ask my friend Tootsie for his recipe for cream-cheese cupcakes. While I was there, I looked at the sundial. Tootsie told me that a mouse in a

motorcycle jacket came to see the sundial just before I did."

"Good work, Trap," Thea said.

My cousin trotted into the kitchen. He came back holding a platter of what seemed to be food. A terrible smell reached my snout.

"Let's celebrate!" he said. "How about some pickled onions smothered in grape jelly? Or anchovies dipped in honey?"

My stomach did a somersault. "No, thank you," I said.

"Are you sure?" Trap asked. "I made a delicious punch to go with it."

"I'm sure you did," I replied. But there was no time to waste on Trap's disgusting snacks. I wanted to try to solve the mystery. I remembered the rhyme in the hidden painting:

ELEVEN PLACES ARE YOURS TO FIND

ELEVEN LETTERS YOU MUST COMBINE

ONE SINGLE WORD WILL GIVE YOU THE KEY

TO SOLVE THE MYSTERY I GIVE TO THEE

I took out my notebook, where I had written down the eleven letters we'd found:

Y I H T B R L A S N U

Lost in thought, I reached for a glass of water. I grabbed the nearest cup and gulped down the contents. I heard Trap mumble, "There goes my glass of SUPER-HOT CHILI PUNCH!"

The eleven letters whirled around in my head.

I didn't feel anything at first. Then, SUDDENLY, my mouth was on fire! I could feel smoke coming out of my ears.

"cheese niblets!" I shrieked.

Maybe it was the sudden shock, but all at once, a single word popped into my head:

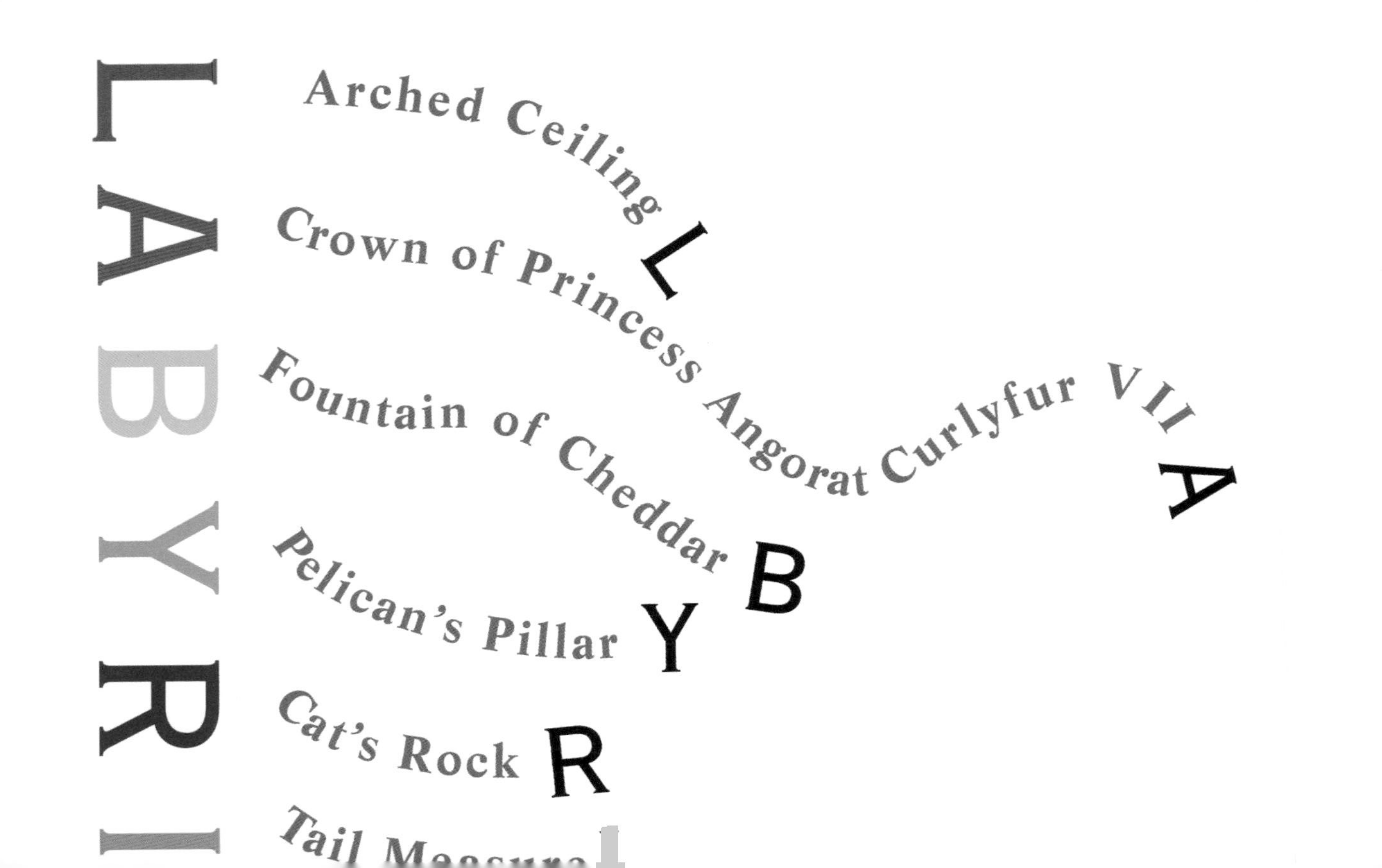
LABYRI
Arched Ceiling
Crown of Princess Angorat Curlyfur VII
Fountain of Cheddar
Pelican's Pillar
Cat's Rock
Tail
L
A
B
Y
R

Pools at the Ancient Baths N

Seal of Mouselius T

Goblet of the Silver Rodent H

Sundial U

Statue of Emeritus Fellowmouse S

NTHUS!

"**Labyrinthus**," I muttered. "Of course! The Labyrinthus was an ancient library. I read about it in a manuscript written by Mousardo da Munchie himself! I have a copy in my private collection."

"Has the **CHILI PUNCH** gone to your head?" Trap asked.

I ignored him. I dashed to my library and found the manuscript. I began reading aloud:

"The Labyrinthus, a great library, stood in the heart of town. It was a **MAZE** of thousands of corridors. The poor soul who entered its hallways might never find the way out! Alas, now our beloved city is threatened by the Great War of the Cats. So I, Mousardo da Munchie, have hidden the Labyrinthus. It once was. It is now no more. But maybe one day it shall be again. . . ."

After the Great War of the Cats, New Mouse City was built over the remains of Old Mouse City. Mousardo said that the Labyrinthus was located in the heart of the old town. . . .

"That could be **Singing Stone Plaza!**" I cried.

"I know where it is!" Thea said. "I'll drive. **Follow me!**"

Thea dashed out. Trap and Benjamin followed her.

As for me, I hopped on my bicycle. I'm too fond of my fur!

The Singing Stone

Singing Stone Plaza is one of the oldest places in town. No one knows why it has such an unusual name. It is paved in stone. Right in the middle stands an obelisk. The tall, THIN pillar seems to touch the sky.

When we arrived, the plaza was deserted. I was excited. "The Labyrinthus has to be here," I said. "I can feel it in my whiskers!"

We examined the square inch by inch. There had to be some clue that would lead us to the Labyrinthus.

We looked for hours, but we didn't find a thing. I started to worry. Could I be wrong?

My cousin was sucking on a Swiss-cheese-flavored lollipop. He shook his head. "There's nothing here. Zilch!

Zip! Nada!" he complained. "I told you that chili punch went to your head!"

"It has to be here," I protested. "Mousardo da Munchie said he hid the **LABYRINTHUS** in the center of town."

"Give it up, Cousin," Trap grumbled. "There is no **LABYRINTHUS**. Maybe Mousardo da Munchie was playing some kind of joke."

"I don't want to give up," I replied. "I feel like we're so close!"

"I think Trap is right," Thea said. "Let's just call it a night, Gerrykins."

But Benjamin did not want to give up. "If Uncle Geronimo says the Labyrinthus is here, then it *must* **be here** somewhere."

Trap snorted. "Take a look around, mouselet," he said. "Do you see any labyrinthuses? I don't."

After what seemed like forever,
he reached the very top.

I felt like crying. We had worked so hard to find all of the clues! Trap must have seen the sad look on my snout, because he stood up.

"Tell you what, Cousinkins," he said. "I'm going to check for you one more time. Maybe we just need a better view."

To my amazement, Trap walked up to the obelisk and began to **climb** it! He shimmied up the pillar like a cat climbing a tree.

"Trap, come down!" I shouted. "It's too dangerous!"

But Trap kept climbing. "You should see the view from here," he called back cheerfully.

Higher and higher he went. I got dizzy just looking at him. After what seemed like forever, he reached the very top.

THERE IS NO LABYRINTHUS!

"Sorry, Cousinkins!" Trap shouted from the top of the obelisk. "There is **no Labyrinthus** ... *inthus* ... *inthus*..."

Trap's voice bounced all over the square.

"It's an echo..." I said. "Maybe that's why it's called Singing Stone Plaza!"

The echo kept repeating: "...inthus ...inthus ...inthus!" It bounced off the bench, the bushes, the stones.

"...inthus ...inthus ...inthus!" The echo grew louder and louder. It really did sound like the square was singing!

"...inthus ...inthus ...inthus!" The echo was so **LOUD**, it made the ground shake under our paws!

"Is it AN EARTHQUAKE?" Thea asked.

"This isn't an earthquake," I said. "The stone circle we are standing on is shifting. We've got to move, FAST!"

Trap slid down the obelisk. I grabbed Benjamin's paw, and we all scurried away as fast as we could.

We reached the edge of the plaza and jumped off just in time. The stone circle was turning upside down! The tall obelisk disappeared into the earth. As the flip side of the square settled into place, a long, gray building appeared. One word was etched in the stone over the door: LABYRINTHUS!

I was so excited! I was right! Mousardo da Munchie had hidden the clues in the *Mona Mousa* painting to keep the location of the

Labyrinthus a secret. But we had found it!

We waited until the square was completely still. Then we approached the Labyrinthus. We pushed open the stone door and found ourselves facing a tangle of dark corridors. They seemed to go on forever. The walls were lined with bookcases full of books.

I SHIVERED. No rodent had set paw in these halls for hundreds of years!

Benjamin grabbed my paw. "Keep close, Uncle," he said. "I'm afraid I'll lose my way."

"Let's tie a piece of string to the front door," Thea said. "We can use it to find our way back to the entrance."

"Excellent idea!" Trap agreed. He grabbed a thread that was hanging from my green cashmere scarf.

"Let's go!" he yelled. Then he ran down one of the halls, holding the thread.

The stone circle was turning upside down!

My scarf began to unravel. Soon it was one very long green thread.

"That was my favorite scarf!" I sighed.

Benjamin stood on his tiptoes and kissed my cheek. "Don't be sad, Uncle. I'll give you my scarf. It's not cashmere like yours, but it's green."

I gave Benjamin a hug. It's easy to see why he is my favorite nephew!

We entered the dark hallway, following the thread. Thea led the way, shining a flashlight. As we walked, I studied the books on the shelves. They were so old! I took book after book off the shelves, blowing the dust off their covers.

I came across one huge book with a leather cover. The title was embossed in GOLD:

THE HISTORY OF MOUSE ISLAND.

Benjamin read the yellowed pages along

My scarf began to unravel.

with me, delighted. We slowly moved deeper into the Labyrinthus, twisting and turning through the halls. Soon it became so dark, we couldn't see the entrance anymore.

"Maybe we should head back," Thea said. "I think we need to turn right."

"No, I think we should turn left," I said.

We turned left. But that only got us more lost. So we turned right. That didn't help, either. We were definitely LOST.

Then Benjamin tugged on my sleeve. "Don't forget about the string, Uncle," he said.

Of course! I was so excited about all of the books, I had forgotten about the string.

Thea, Benjamin, and I retraced our steps, winding the ball into a string as we walked. Trap was nowhere in sight.

Soon it was one very long green thread.

No rodent had set paw in these halls
for hundreds of years!

"I hope he isn't lost," I said, worried.

Finally, we reached the entrance. **ALL OF A SUDDEN**, a strange sound came through the darkness.

Crunch . . . crunch . . . crunch . . .

I was so *scared*, I almost *jumped* out of my fur. Had someone else found the Labyrinthus?

A dark figure came toward us through the shadows.

"Hi, Cousinkins," Trap said. He was munching on a bag of blue cheese chips.

I sighed with relief. "It's only you," I said.

But then I heard another sound.

CREAK . . . CREAK . . . CREAK . . .

"Trap?" I asked nervously.

"Not me," Trap whispered. "I finished my chips."

That could only mean one thing. Someone else was in the Labyrinthus!

SPILL THE BEANS, CHEDDARFACE!

We quickly hid behind a bookshelf. Thea turned off her flashlight.

"SSH! Nobody make a sound!" I whispered.

Creak . . . creak . . . creak. The sounds got closer and closer. From our hiding place, we could see a **flashlight** moving in the **darkness.** A mouse-shaped shadow loomed on the wall.

"HE'S MINE," Trap whispered. "JUST WATCH!"

Trap leaped out and grabbed the intruder by the tail.

"Got you, **FURBRAIN!**" Trap yelled.

We all jumped out from behind the shelf. Thea turned on her flashlight. She aimed

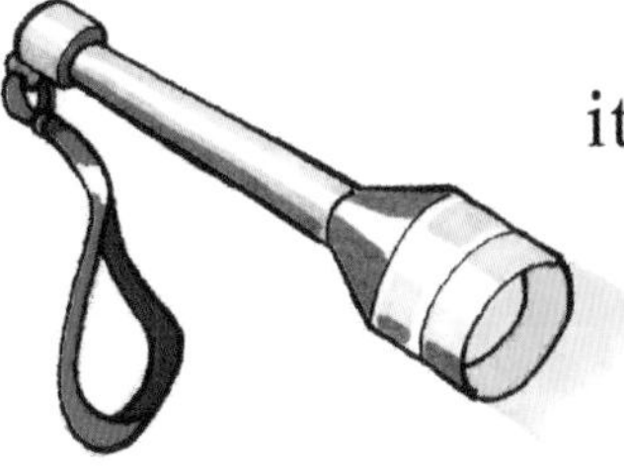

it at the intruder.

"Let's see who you are, *you rat fink!*" she shouted.

The light shone on a long and narrow snout. A pair of gold-rimmed glasses. A blue bow tie and a red vest . . .

"Simeon Starchfur!" I cried. The distinguished curator of the mouseum was sneaking around after us! I was stunned.

Trap had Simeon in a headlock. The curator waved his paws wildly, *trying to speak*.

"Spill the beans, *Cheddarface*," Trap said. "Where are all of those mysterious mice who were helping you?"

"Let him go, Trap," I said. "I think he wants to say something."

Trap loosened his grip. Simeon swallowed,

gasping for air. "Painting . . ." he gasped. "Council . . . investigation . . ."

"**What, what, what?**" Thea asked. "Sounds like you've got a frog in your throat. I can't hear you. Squeak up!"

Simeon fumbled in his vest. He took out a piece of paper covered with official-looking stamps. He handed it to Thea. She read it aloud.

"'The Great Council of Mouse Island instructs **Simeon Starchfur**, esteemed curator of our mouseum, to undertake a SECRET INVESTIGATION of the picture hidden under the *Mona Mousa*.'"

I grabbed the paper in disbelief. "THE GREAT COUNCIL?" I asked. Those important rodents called all the shots on Mouse Island.

Simeon nodded. "When Frick Tapioca discovered another painting under the *Mona Mousa*, I knew it was an *important discovery*," he began. "I also knew it should remain secret. I asked the Great Council for permission to investigate. Then I traveled all over Mouse Island, looking for the eleven letters. What a struggle! I didn't figure out that the key word was **Labyrinthus** until tonight."

Trap looked sheepish. "Um, does that mean I have to let him go?"

I nodded, and Trap released the curator. Simeon dusted off his vest and straightened his glasses.

"That's some grip you've got there, young mouse," he said, rubbing his neck.

Trap was still suspicious. "If you wanted to keep things a secret, then who were those

mysterious mice following us around?" he asked. "There was that **clown**. And the mouse in motorcycle gear. And the widow wearing a veil."

He took a piece of paper from his pocket. It showed Thea's drawings of all eleven suspects.

An old lady with a basket of apples

A widow wearing a veil

A Roman gladiator

Simeon smiled. "There is no one else," he said. "**I'm** the one you're looking for!"

He opened his briefcase. Inside was a jumble of disguises!

"Here is the helmet worn by the motorcycle mouse," he said, holding it up. "And here is the clown's wig, and the

Who were those mysterious mice?

A mouse wearing a pair of floral pants and another wearing a striped vest

widow's veil. I bought everything at a shop that sells **tricks and costumes**."

Trap inspected the contents of the briefcase. Then he grinned and slapped Simeon on the back. "I know where you got

A clown with a wig

A cute mouse dressed as Little Red Riding Hood

A mouse wear a raincoat

this stuff," he said, chuckling. "At Tricks for Tails, my favorite joke shop! We should go together sometime. My friend Paws Prankster will give us a **discount**."

A First-Rat Story

A month has gone by since we discovered the **Labyrinthus**. You won't believe everything that has happened since *then*!

First of all, the Labyrinthus has been turned into a mouseum. Thousands of rodents visit every day. It makes me so happy to know that mice all over Mouse Island are enjoying those rare books.

But that's not all. There is another piece of news. Can you guess where I am right now? I'll tell you. I'm on the set of a new movie, *The Mona Mousa Code.* Can you guess who's directing it? Steven Spielmouse himself! It's a film version of the book written by yours truly, Geronimo Stilton. Right now, it's **number one** on the bestseller list.

I knew this would be a

FIRST-RAT STORY!

It's a film version of the book written
by yours truly, Geronimo Stilton.

I'M TOO FOND OF MY FUR

Tonight is a special occasion. The mouseum is going to present Thea, Trap, Benjamin, and me with an award. It's every mouse's dream: the **GOLDEN RIND**!

Cheesecake! *I'm so happy*. This is better than winning the mouse lotto.

Last night, I was so excited, I didn't sleep a wink. I got dressed hours ago. It's a formal ceremony, so I'm wearing my tuxedo. I have been pacing ***back and forth*** across my room. I can't wait for the ceremony to start!

Thea calls me from the next room.

"Geronimo, are you ready?"

"Yes!" I answer, running out. Thea is standing there in her gown, holding the keys to her sports car. She opens the door, hops into the car, and **takes off** . . . alone!

I leave my mouse hole and walk to the subway station. It will be crowded at this time of day, but I don't care.

I'm too fond of my fur!

About the Author

Born in New Mouse City, Mouse Island, **Geronimo Stilton** is Rattus Emeritus of Mousomorphic Literature and of Neo-Ratonic Comparative Philosophy. For the past twenty years, he has been running *The Rodent's Gazette*, New Mouse City's most widely read daily newspaper.

Stilton was awarded the Ratitzer Prize for his scoops on *The Curse of the Cheese Pyramid* and *The Search for Sunken Treasure*. He has also received the Andersen 2000 Prize for Personality of the Year. One of his bestsellers won the 2002 eBook Award for world's best ratlings' electronic book. His works have been published all over the globe.

In his spare time, Mr. Stilton collects antique cheese rinds and plays golf. But what he most enjoys is telling stories to his nephew Benjamin.

Want to read my next adventure?
It's sure to be a fur-raising experience!

Surf's Up, Geronimo!

Geronimo Stilton has ducked out of the rat race for a quiet holiday in the sun. But instead of a beautiful seaside resort he finds himself in a fleabag hotel that's falling down around his ears! Will he be able to enjoy a relaxing break or is it holiday horrors all round?

Don't miss any of my fabumouse adventures!

1
2
3
4
5
6
7
8
9
10
11
12
13
14
15
16
17
18
19
20
21
22
23
24
25
26
27
28
29
30
31
32
33
34
35
36
37
38
39
40
41
42
43
44
45
46
RODENT RIVER
Beach

Map of New Mouse City

1. Industrial Zone
2. Cheese Factories
3. Angorat International Airport
4. WRAT Radio and Television Station
5. Cheese Market
6. Fish Market
7. Town Hall
8. Snotnose Castle
9. The Seven Hills of Mouse Island
10. Mouse Central Station
11. Trade Center
12. Movie Theater
13. Gym
14. Catnegie Hall
15. Singing Stone Plaza
16. The Gouda Theater
17. Grand Hotel
18. Mouse General Hospital
19. Botanical Gardens
20. Cheap Junk for Less (Trap's store)
21. Parking Lot
22. Mouseum of Modern Art
23. University and Library
24. *The Daily Rat*
25. *The Rodent's Gazette*
26. Trap's House
27. Fashion District
28. The Mouse House Restaurant
29. Environmental Protection Center
30. Harbor Office
31. Mousidon Square Garden
32. Golf Course
33. Swimming Pool
34. Blushing Meadow Tennis Courts
35. Curlyfur Island Amusement Park
36. Geronimo's House
37. Historic District
38. Public Library
39. Shipyard
40. Thea's House
41. New Mouse Harbor
42. Luna Lighthouse
43. The Statue of Liberty
44. Hercule Poirat's Office
45. Petunia Pretty Paws's House
46. Grandfather William's House

This way to the Rodent Straits
Brigand's Isle
Tomcat Island
Pirate Ship of Cats
Hamster Islands
Blue Dolphin Bay
Cat's Claw Bay
Panther Archipelago
Coral Reefs
This way to the Mousific Ocean
Stray Cat Harbor
Swissville
Cheddarton
Mouseport
San Mouscisco
This way to the Ratlantic Ocean
New Mouse City
Mousefort Beach
Furflung Island
This way to the Sea of Mice
MOUSE ISLAND
N
W
E
S
1
2
3
4
5
6
7
8
9
10
11
12
13
14
15
16
17
18
19
20
21
22
23
24
25
26
27
28
29
30
31
32
33
34
35
36
37

Map of Mouse Island

1. Big Ice Lake
2. Frozen Fur Peak
3. Slipperyslopes Glacier
4. Coldcreeps Peak
5. Ratzikistan
6. Transratania
7. Mount Vamp
8. Roastedrat Volcano
9. Brimstone Lake
10. Poopedcat Pass
11. Stinko Peak
12. Dark Forest
13. Vain Vampires Valley
14. Goose Bumps Gorge
15. The Shadow Line Pass
16. Penny Pincher Castle
17. Nature Reserve Park
18. Las Ratayas Marinas
19. Fossil Forest
20. Lake Lake
21. Lake Lakelake
22. Lake Lakelakelake
23. Cheddar Crag
24. Cannycat Castle
25. Valley of the Giant Sequoia
26. Cheddar Springs
27. Sulfurous Swamp
28. Old Reliable Geyser
29. Vole Vale
30. Ravingrat Ravine
31. Gnat Marshes
32. Munster Highlands
33. Mousehara Desert
34. Oasis of the Sweaty Camel
35. Cabbagehead Hill
36. Rattytrap Jungle
37. Rio Mosquito

Geronimo Stilton